# Dear Parents:

Congratulations! Your child is taking the first steps on an exciting journey. The destination? Independent reading!

**STEP INTO READING®** will help your child get there. The program offers five steps to reading success. Each step includes fun stories and colorful art or photographs. In addition to original fiction and books with favorite characters, there are Step into Reading Non-Fiction Readers, Phonics Readers and Boxed Sets, Sticker Readers, and Comic Readers—a complete literacy program with something to interest every child.

## Learning to Read, Step by Step!

### Ready to Read    Preschool–Kindergarten
• big type and easy words • rhyme and rhythm • picture clues
For children who know the alphabet and are eager to begin reading.

### Reading with Help    Preschool–Grade 1
• basic vocabulary • short sentences • simple stories
For children who recognize familiar words and sound out new words with help.

### Reading on Your Own    Grades 1–3
• engaging characters • easy-to-follow plots • popular topics
For children who are ready to read on their own.

### Reading Paragraphs    Grades 2–3
• challenging vocabulary • short paragraphs • exciting stories
For newly independent readers who read simple sentences with confidence.

### Ready for Chapters    Grades 2–4
• chapters • longer paragraphs • full-color art
For children who want to take the plunge into chapter books but still like colorful pictures.

**STEP INTO READING®** is designed to give every child a successful reading experience. The grade levels are only guides; children will progress through the steps at their own speed, developing confidence in their reading.

Remember, a lifetime love of reading starts with a single step!

Published in the United States by Random House Children's Books, a division of Penguin Random House
LLC, 1745 Broadway, New York, NY 10019, and in Canada by Penguin Random House Canada Limited,
Toronto.

Step into Reading, Random House, and the Random House colophon are registered trademarks of
Penguin Random House LLC.

Visit us on the Web!
StepIntoReading.com
rhcbooks.com

Educators and librarians, for a variety of teaching tools, visit us at RHTeachersLibrarians.com

ISBN 978-0-593-56403-5 (trade)
ISBN 978-0-593-56404-2 (lib. bdg.)
ISBN 978-0-593-56405-9 (ebook)

Printed in the United States of America
10 9 8 7 6 5 4 3 2 1

LEGO DC SUPER HEROES

# PENGUIN TROUBLE!

based on the story "The Penguin's Zoo Takeover!"
by Liz Marsham

illustrated by AMEET Studio

Random House 🏠 New York

Batman swings
over Gotham City.
He is always
on the lookout
for trouble.
And there is always trouble
in Gotham City. . . .

Batman gets a call
in the Batcave,
his secret hideout.
Something is happening
at the new Gotham City Zoo.

*CRASH!*

The animals smash
through the gates
of the zoo!

They escape and run
down the street.

# Even the cute penguins get away!

Batman needs help
to round up
the animals.
He alerts his friends
in the Justice League.

The super-fast
Super Hero
The Flash says
he is on the way!
*Whoosh!*

The Super Heroes
quickly arrive
at the zoo.
There are
Supergirl, Batgirl,
Batman, Aquaman,
and Green Lantern!

The Flash leaves a trail
of tasty treats
for the black panther
to follow back to the zoo.

Batman and the other
Super Heroes
move the bigger animals,
like the elephants
and the giraffes,
safely back
where they belong.

The next day,
Batman gets an alert
that The Penguin
is causing trouble—
with an army of penguins!

Batman calls Aquaman
and asks him about
the penguins at the zoo.
Oh, no!
Aquaman realizes
he forgot to bring
in the penguins!

Batman follows
the trail of crimes
to an underground base.
He sees a strange device
that was built
by The Penguin.

The Penguin is using
the device to make
the penguins
steal for him.

Batman is trapped!
The Penguin
and his army
tie Batman up.

The villain says the penguins
will help him rob
every jewelry store
in Gotham City—
and maybe the world!

Batman's friends arrive
just in time.
They take The Penguin's
device apart.
The bad guy
tries to run away.
He will not get far.

# Dear Parents:

Congratulations! Your child is taking the first steps on an exciting journey. The destination? Independent reading!

**STEP INTO READING®** will help your child get there. The program offers five steps to reading success. Each step includes fun stories and colorful art or photographs. In addition to original fiction and books with favorite characters, there are Step into Reading Non-Fiction Readers, Phonics Readers and Boxed Sets, Sticker Readers, and Comic Readers—a complete literacy program with something to interest every child.

## Learning to Read, Step by Step!

**1**

### Ready to Read  Preschool–Kindergarten
• big type and easy words • rhyme and rhythm • picture clues
For children who know the alphabet and are eager to begin reading.

**2**

### Reading with Help  Preschool–Grade 1
• basic vocabulary • short sentences • simple stories
For children who recognize familiar words and sound out new words with help.

**3**

### Reading on Your Own  Grades 1–3
• engaging characters • easy-to-follow plots • popular topics
For children who are ready to read on their own.

**4**

### Reading Paragraphs  Grades 2–3
• challenging vocabulary • short paragraphs • exciting stories
For newly independent readers who read simple sentences with confidence.

**5**

### Ready for Chapters  Grades 2–4
• chapters • longer paragraphs • full-color art
For children who want to take the plunge into chapter books but still like colorful pictures.

**STEP INTO READING®** is designed to give every child a successful reading experience. The grade levels are only guides; children will progress through the steps at their own speed, developing confidence in their reading.

Remember, a lifetime love of reading starts with a single step!

Published in the United States by Random House Children's Books, a division of Penguin Random House
LLC, 1745 Broadway, New York, NY 10019, and in Canada by Penguin Random House Canada Limited,
Toronto.

Step into Reading, Random House, and the Random House colophon are registered trademarks of
Penguin Random House LLC.

Visit us on the Web!
StepIntoReading.com
rhcbooks.com

Educators and librarians, for a variety of teaching tools, visit us at RHTeachersLibrarians.com

ISBN 978-0-593-56403-5 (trade)
ISBN 978-0-593-56404-2 (lib. bdg.)
ISBN 978-0-593-56405-9 (ebook)

Printed in the United States of America
10 9 8 7 6 5 4 3 2 1

# FLASH FORWARD!

based on the story "Super-Villain Ghost Scare!"
by Liz Marsham
illustrated by AMEET Studio

Random House 🏠 New York

The Flash
is the Fastest Man Alive!
He can get to the scene
of any crime super-fast
and take on any bad guy
with his super-speed.
*WHOOSH!*

Batman, The Flash,
Batgirl, Supergirl,
and Superman
are called to the city's
Super Hero Museum.
It is being haunted
by ghosts!

Superman and Supergirl
take on some of the ghosts.

The ghosts are no match

for the Super Heroes.

One ghost smashes
on the ground.
It is not a ghost.
It is a robot!

The Flash races past
the robot ghosts
and runs into the museum.

The Flash sees
his enemy—
Reverse Flash.
Reverse Flash
is trying to steal
the Time Treadmill!

Moving super-fast,
The Flash grabs a piece
of the machine
and runs!

# Reverse Flash chases The Flash.

He wants the part back,
but The Flash is too fast.

The Flash leads
Reverse Flash
through the museum.

The exhibits include some of the greatest Super Hero battles.

The Flash tricks
Reverse Flash into
entering a hall of mirrors.

Reverse Flash
is trapped!
The Flash goes
to find his friends.

Just then, Batman
swings into the museum.
He tells The Flash to lead
Reverse Flash out the door.
The Super Heroes
have built a trap!

When The Flash runs out,
Supergirl tosses him
into the air
and over the trap.

Reverse Flash chases
The Flash.

He is running so fast,
he does not see the trap.

Got him!

Batman, The Flash, and the Super Heroes have used teamwork to stop the bad guy!

The penguins are now safe.
Batman and his friends
will return them to the zoo . . .
and take The Penguin to jail!